COOKIE MONSTER AND THE COOKIE TREE

by DAVID KORR
illustrated by JOE MATHIEU

Featuring Jim Henson's Muppets

This educational book was created in cooperation with the Children's Television Workshop, producers of Sesame Street. Children do not have to watch the television show to benefit from this book. Workshop revenues from this product will be used to help support CTW educational projects.

A SESAME STREET BOOK

Published by Western Publishing Company, Inc. in conjunction with Children's Television Workshop. © 1977 Children's Television Workshop. Cookie Monster and other Muppet characters © 1971, 1972, 1973, 1977 Muppets, Inc. All rights reserved. Produced in U.S.A. Sesame Street® and the Sesame Street sign are trademarks and service marks of Children's Television Workshop. Cookie Monster is a trademark of Muppets, Inc. GOLDEN®, A GOLDEN BOOK®, and GOLDEN PRESS® are trademarks of Western Publishing Company, Inc. No part of this book may be reproduced or copied in any form without written permission from the publisher.

0-307-10821-X

Weekly Reader Children's Book Club Presents

Weekly Reader Books offers several exciting card and activity programs.
For information, write to WEEKLY READER BOOKS, P.O. Box 16636, Columbus, Ohio 43216.

One day (it was a Tuesday, but that doesn't matter), a witch (who wasn't a very clever witch, and that *does* matter) was out in the forest visiting her cookie tree.

Library of Congress Cataloging in Publication Data
Korr, David.
    Cookie Monster and the cookie tree.

    "A Sesame Street book."
    "Created in cooperation with the Children's Television
Workshop, producers of Sesame Street."
    SUMMARY: Cookie Monster and a clever, selfish witch
are forced into a seemingly impossible situation:
sharing cookies.
    [1. Cookies—Fiction. 2. Sharing—Fiction.
3. Monsters—Fiction. 4. Witches—Fiction]
I. Mathieu, Joseph. II. Children's Television Workshop. IV. Title.
PZ7.K8375Co 1979   [E]   79-10796

The witch was very fond of her cookie tree.
She was also very selfish.

She was just about to eat a cookie, when all of a sudden, she saw trouble coming.

Now, to you and me, the Cookie Monster might not seem like trouble. But for someone who has a cookie tree, it's a different story. The witch decided she'd better cast a magic spell on the tree so that it wouldn't let the Cookie Monster have any cookies.

Then the witch hid in the bushes to see if her spell would work.

Cookie Monster could hardly believe his eyes. *"Cookie* tree?" he wondered. He went very close for a better look. "Look like cookies," he said.

He listened to one. "Sound like cookies," he said.

He smelled one. "Smell like cookies!"

He touched one. *"Feel* like cookies!"

Then he tried to taste one.

The tree pulled all the cookies
out of his reach.

HEY,
WHAT YOU
DOING ?

The tree told him. "I am a magic cookie tree, and I only give
cookies to people who will share them."

"That silly," said the Cookie Monster. *Me* not share cookies.
Gimme cookie!"

"No," said the tree. "That's the rule. You have to have someone to share with."

"Oh, all right," said Cookie Monster. "Me go get someone to share cookie with. You wait here. Don't go away."

The Cookie Monster ran all the way back to Sesame Street, where he saw his friend Herry Monster. "Herry," he said, "old furry old pal, come with me to cookie tree. Hurry. Me need someone to share cookies with."

But Herry didn't believe him.

Next, the Cookie Monster saw Big Bird. "Oh, Big Bird," he said. "You want some cookies? Me need someone to share them with." Big Bird didn't believe him, either.

WHAT? ARE YOU FEELING ALL RIGHT, COOKIE MONSTER?

Cookie Monster was getting discouraged. "But," he said, "me not give up."

Meanwhile, back at the cookie tree, the witch was having problems of her own. When she tried to take a cookie, the magic tree said to her, "Stop. You can't have one. You told me to give cookies only to people who will *share* them."

"But I didn't mean *me!*"

said the witch.

And what about Cookie Monster? Well, he was still trying to find someone to share the cookies with him.

Now Cookie Monster was even more discouraged. "Oh, please," he said, "somebody believe me!"

But no one did.

So, feeling sad and hungry, the Cookie Monster walked back
through the forest to see if the cookie tree would change its mind.

And what was the witch doing all this time? She was *still* trying to get a cookie.

When Cookie Monster heard the witch and the tree arguing, he knew who had caused all the trouble.

Cookie Monster had an idea. "Hey! You and me can share cookie," he told the witch.

"Say," she said, "that's so crazy it just might work."

So they tried it.

"Okay," said the tree and lowered its branches. Cookie Monster took a cookie and broke it into two pieces, one for himself and one for the witch.

And then they shared it.